The Girl who owned a Bear

and other stories

Miles
KeLLY

First published in 2011 by Miles Kelly Publishing Ltd
Harding's Barn, Bardfield End Green, Thaxted, Essex, CM6 3PX, UK

2 4 6 8 10 9 7 5 3 1

Publishing Director Belinda Gallagher

Creative Director Jo Cowan

Editor Amanda Askew

Senior Designer Joe Jones

Designer Kayleigh Allen

Production Manager Elizabeth Collins

Reprographics Anthony Cambray, Stephan Davis, Jennifer Hunt

ISBN 978-1-84810-439-6

Printed in China

British Library Cataloguing-in-Publication Data
A catalogue record for this book is available from the British Library

ACKNOWLEDGEMENTS
Artworks are from the Miles Kelly Artwork Bank

Made with paper from a sustainable forest

www.mileskelly.net
info@mileskelly.net

www.factsforprojects.com

Self-publish your
children's book

buddingpress.co.uk

Contents

The Thunder God gets Married

A Norse legend

Up in heaven, Thor the thunder god was
furious. Someone had stolen his magic
hammer. Thor's magic hammer was the terror of
the gods. Whenever he threw it, it killed anything
that it touched and it always returned to his hand.
It was perhaps the most deadly weapon that the
gods possessed to protect them against their
enemies, the giants.

Now the raging Thor's roaring sounded like the

clouds were clashing together. His face was so black with anger that it sent a dark shadow over the whole sky. As Thor grabbed blazing lightning bolts and hurled them, the mischief-maker god, Loki, came nervously to see him.

"I have good news, my angry friend," Loki explained. "I have used my cunning to find out that it is the giant Thrym who has stolen your hammer. He has agreed to give it back on one condition – that he has the most beautiful of all the goddesses, Freya, as his bride."

The thunder god's sulky face brightened a little and he charged off to find Freya straight away.

"Put on your best dress, Freya!" Thor boomed, throwing open her wardrobe doors. "You have to marry the giant Thrym so I can get my magic hammer back."

Freya's eyes flickered with cold fire. "Excuse me,

Thor," she said, calmly. "Would you care to repeat that?"

"You-have-to-marry-the-giant-Thrym-so-I-can-get-my-magic-hammer-back!" the impatient thunder god cried at top speed.

Freya stood glaring, her hands on her hips. "Firstly Thor, as the goddess of beauty I don't have to do anything." Thor's face reddened.

"Secondly," Freya continued, "I wouldn't marry that ugly monster Thrym if he were the only creature left in the world." The ashamed thunder god hung his head.

"Thirdly," Freya finished, "it's your problem, you sort it out."

"Sorry, Freya," Thor mumbled, shuffling about

a bit. Then he turned and stormed back to Loki. The two gods sat down glumly and wracked their brains to come up with another way to get back the hammer.

"How about…" Thor started to suggest. Then he shook his head. "No, no good."

"What if…" Loki began. Then his face fell. "No, it would never work."

It looked as if Thor's magic hammer would have to stay in the land of the giants forever — until the god Heimdall had an idea.

"That's absolutely out of the question!" Thor thundered.

"Outrageous!" Loki squealed. "I'll never do it!"

"Well, you come up with another plan then," Heimdall laughed, knowing that there wasn't one.

That night, the giant Thrym was delighted to see a chariot with a bride and bridesmaid in it rumbling up to his castle.

"It's Freya!" the gormless giant gasped with delight. "I shall gladly give back Thor's magic hammer in return for the most beautiful wife in the world!" The overjoyed giant commanded a magnificent banquet to be prepared and his guests to be sent for at once.

But Thrym wouldn't have been so overjoyed if he could have seen what was underneath the veils of his bride and bridesmaid – the angry, highly embarrassed faces of Thor and Loki! As it was, the giant was far too excited to notice how big and clumsy the bride and bridesmaid looked in their frilly dresses. Thrym didn't take in that the women had low, gruff voices and huge, hairy hands. And he hardly thought twice about the way that Freya swigged down two whole barrels of beer and ate an entire roast ox.

When the guests had eaten and drunk their fill, the beaming Thrym stood up to make a speech.

"My wife and I," he began, blushing bright red, "would like to thank you for celebrating this happy occasion with us. Freya has made me the luckiest being in the whole universe. And now, I will keep my word and give back the magic hammer I stole from that ugly thug of a thunder god."

There was a roll of drums as one of Thrym's servants brought in the magic hammer on a cushion. Thrym held it high in the air for his marvelling guests to admire. Then with a grand flourish, he presented it to his bride.

"The ugly thug of a thunder god thanks you!" roared Thor, ripping off his veil and springing to his feet. And before Thrym and his guests could really take in the trick, they were lying dead on the floor and the wedding feast was unexpectedly over.

All the gods were truly relieved to have the magic hammer back in Thor's hands in heaven, where it belonged. But it was a long time before Thor and Loki could laugh with the other gods about how charming they both looked in a dress!

The Wonderful Tar Baby

By Uncle Remus

Brer Fox was doing what he usually did —
trying to catch Brer Rabbit. But he'd be
danged if this time he didn't catch that pesky
varmint once and for all! Brer Fox mixed up a big
pot of sticky tar and pulled and patted it into the
shape of a baby. Then he lolloped up the road, set
the tar baby sitting in the dust, and went to lay
low in the ditch.

By and by, Brer Rabbit came bouncing down

the road. "Good morning," he greeted the tar baby, "nice day, ain't it?"

But the tar baby didn't utter a word.

"I SAYS," shouted Brer Rabbit, just in case the tar baby hadn't cleaned his ears recently, "GOOD MORNING! NICE DAY, AIN'T IT?"

The tar baby just stared straight ahead.

"Ain't you got no manners?" Brer Rabbit asked, crossly.

Still the tar baby stayed silent.

By this time, Brer Rabbit was hopping from foot to foot, madder than a snake in a wasps' nest. "You'd better speak to me civil-like or else!" he hollered.

But the tar baby simply ignored Brer Rabbit.

"Well I guess you've done gone and asked for this!" Brer Rabbit shrieked.

BLIP! He thumped the tar baby straight in the mouth – and his fist was stuck fast to the tar baby's face. "You let me go!" Brer Rabbit yelled. "Let me go – or I'll let you have another!"

BLAM! Brer Rabbit socked the tar baby again and his other fist became glued to its head.

SMACK! He kicked the tar baby and was left hopping around on one leg.

WALLOP! another kick and the tar baby was holding him off the ground. "Right, you've really had it now!" Brer Rabbit screamed.

THUNK! he headbutted the tar baby and found himself stuck eye-to-eye.

All this time, Brer Fox had been holding on to so much laughter he thought he was going to burst. He leapt out of his hiding place and howled, "My, oh my, Brer Rabbit! What type of mess have you got yourself into this time?"

"I suppose you're gonna have a tasty barbecued bunny for supper," Brer Rabbit admitted.

"Yep!" grinned Brer Fox, licking his lips.

"Well I'm glad you're going to dress me up with some sauce and warm me over your fire," Brer Rabbit smiled. "I'd much rather you did that than throw me in that briar patch over there."

Hang on a minute, thought Brer Fox, and his face fell. That no-good rabbit seems quite pleased about being roasted! "I've changed my mind," Brer Fox said. "I'm gonna hang you instead."

"Ain't I glad it's good ol' hangin' and not being thrown in the briar patch!" sighed Brer Rabbit.

Brer Fox frowned. "I mean, I'm going to drown you!" he snarled.

"Fine, fine," smiled Brer Rabbit gaily. "Dip me in the water and at least I'll die clean. Just don't throw me in that there briar patch, that's all!"

At that, Brer Fox was sure that the very worst thing he could do to Brer Rabbit was to hurl him into the briar patch. He grabbed him round the waist and pulled him hard and – SHLUP! – Brer Rabbit came unstuck from the tar baby. Brer Fox spun round and round and – WHEEEEEEEE! – Brer Rabbit went sailing high into the air and came down – DONK! – into the briar patch.

Brer Fox began to smile contentedly. "I've bested that bunny once and for all!" he chuckled.

A high-pitched giggle came from the far side of the briar patch, and when Brer Fox squinted into the sunshine, he could just see Brer Rabbit hopping away into the distance. "I was born and bred in a briar patch, Brer Fox!" he was singing.

Brer Fox boiled with rage and thumped the very first thing that came to hand. And you know what that was, don't you?

The Clever Apprentice

By Walter Gregor

A shoemaker once engaged an apprentice. A short time after the apprenticeship began the shoemaker asked the boy what he would call him when addressing him.

"I would call you master," answered the apprentice. "No," said the master, "you must call me master above all masters.

"What would you call my trousers?" "I would call them trousers," said the apprentice. "No, you

16

must call them struntifers."

"And what would you call my wife?" "I would call her mistress," replied the apprentice. "No, you must call her the Fair Lady Permoumadam."

"What would you call my son?" "I would call him Johnny," answered the apprentice. "No, you must call him John the Great."

"And what would you call the cat?" "I would call him pussy." "No, you must call him Great Carle Gropus."

"And what would you call the fire?" "Oh, I would call it fire." "No, you must call it Fire Evangelist."

"And what would you call the peat stack?" "Oh, I would just call it peat stack." "No, you must call it Mount Potago."

"And what would you call the well?" "Oh, I would call it well." "No, you must call it the Fair Fountain."

"And, last of all, what would you call the house?" "Oh, I would call it house." "No, you must call it the Castle of Mungo."

The shoemaker, after giving this lesson to his apprentice, told him that the first day he managed to use all these words at once, without making a mistake, the apprenticeship would end.

Then one morning, the apprentice got out of bed before his master and lit the fire. He tied some bits of paper to the tail of the cat and threw the animal into the fire. The cat ran out with the papers all in a blaze, landed in the peat stack, which caught fire.

The apprentice hurried to his master and cried...

Master above all masters, start up and jump into your struntifers, and call upon Sir John the Great and the Fair Lady Permoumaddam, for Carle Gropus has caught hold of Fire Evangelist, and he is out to Mount Potago, and if you don't get help from the Fair Fountain, the whole of Castle Mungo will be burned to the ground!

The Fairies and the Envious Neighbour

By Algernon Freeman-Mitford

Once upon a time there was a man, who after getting lost in the dark, sheltered in the trunk of a hollow tree. In the middle of the night, a large group of fairies appeared, and the man, peeping out from his hiding place, was frightened out of his wits. After a while, the fairies began to eat and drink, sing and dance. The man, wanting to join in the fun, forgot all about his fright, and crept out of his hollow tree to join in.

 19

As the sun began to rise, the fairies said to the man, "You're very jolly and must come out and dance with us again. Promise us." So, to make sure the man would return, the elves took a large wart that grew on his forehead and kept it.

The man left for his house in glee, both at having passed a great night, and getting rid of his wart. He told the story to all his friends, who were pleased that he was cured of his wart.

His neighbour, who was also troubled with a wart, was jealous, and went to find the hollow tree.

Towards midnight the fairies came, as he had expected, and began feasting and drinking, with songs and dances as before. As soon as he saw this, he came out of his hollow tree, and began dancing and singing as his neighbour had done. The fairies, thinking he was the first man, were delighted to see him, and said, "You're a good fellow to keep your promise, so we'll give you back your wart." With that, one of the fairies pulled the wart out of his pocket, and stuck it onto the man's forehead, on the top of the other wart that he already had.

The envious neighbour went home weeping, with two warts instead of one. This is a good lesson... people should be pleased for the good luck of others, without wanting it for themselves.

Iktomi and the Muskrat

By Zitkala-sa

Beside a white lake, beneath a large willow tree, sat Iktomi the fairy with a pot of boiled fish. He quickly tucked in, for he was hungry.

"How, how, my friend!" said a voice.

Iktomi jumped and almost choked on his soup. He peered through the long reeds from where he sat with his spoon in mid-air.

"How, my friend!" said the voice again, this time at his side. Iktomi turned and there stood a

 22

dripping-wet muskrat.

"Oh, it is my friend who scared me. I wondered if a spirit voice was talking. How, how, my friend!" said Iktomi. The muskrat stood smiling, waiting for Iktomi to ask, 'My friend, will you sit down beside me and share my food?'

Yet Iktomi sat, silent. He hummed an old song and beat gently on the pot with his spoon. The muskrat began to feel awkward and wished himself underwater.

After many minutes, Iktomi stopped drumming with his spoon, and looking upward into the muskrat's face, he said, "My friend, let us run a race to see who shall win this pot of fish. If I win, I shall not need to share it with you. If you win, you shall have half of it." Springing to his feet, Iktomi began at once to tighten the belt about his waist.

"My friend Iktomi, I cannot run a race with you!

I am not a swift runner, and you are nimble as a deer," answered the hungry muskrat.

"Then I shall carry a large stone on my back. That will slow down my usual speed, and the race will be a fair one." Saying this he laid a firm hand upon the muskrat's shoulder and walked to the edge of the lake. When they reached the opposite side, Iktomi searched for a heavy stone. He found one half buried in the shallow water. Pulling it onto dry land, he wrapped it in his blanket.

"Now, my friend, you shall run on the left side of the lake, I on the other. The race is for the boiled fish in yonder kettle!" said Iktomi.

The muskrat helped to lift the heavy stone upon Iktomi's back. Then they parted. Each took a narrow path through the tall reeds on the shore. Iktomi found his load a heavy one. He puffed and panted, and sweat dripped from his forehead.

He looked across the lake to see how far the muskrat had got, but there was no sign of him.

"Well, he is running low under the wild rice!" said he. Yet as he searched the tall grasses on the lake shore, he saw nothing moving.

"Ah, has he gone so fast ahead that the disturbed grasses in his trail have already become quiet again?" exclaimed Iktomi. With that thought he quickly dropped the heavy stone.

"No more of this!" said he, patting his chest with both hands. Off with a springing bound, he ran swiftly towards the goal. Tufts of reeds and grass fell flat under his feet.

Soon he reached the heap of cold ashes. Iktomi halted stiff as if he had struck an invisible cliff. His black eyes showed a ring of white about them as he stared at the empty ground. There was no pot of boiled fish! There was no muskrat in sight!

"Oh, if only I had shared my food, I would not have lost it all! Why did I not remember the muskrat would run through the water? He swims faster than I could ever run! That is what he has done. He has laughed at me for carrying a weight on my back while he shot here like an arrow!"

"Ha! Ha! Ha!" laughed the muskrat. "Next time, say to a visiting friend, 'Be seated beside me, my friend. Let me share my food with you.'"

Amal and the Genie

A Persian fairytale

Many moons ago in ancient Persia there lived a bright young man called Amal. He was out one day when he had the misfortune to meet a genie. Now sometimes genies can be good news, but this one was in a very bad temper and he was looking for trouble. Amal had to think quickly. He had no weapons with him, only an egg and a lump of salt in his pocket.

The genie came whirling up to Amal, but before

27

he could say anything, Amal yelled at him.

"Genie! You and I should have a competition to see who is the strongest!"

You might think this was very foolish of Amal, but he knew two things about genies. One was that it is always better to take control first, and the second was that genies are not terribly bright. They are fine at conjuring up gorgeous palaces and flying carpets, but they are a bit slow when it comes to basic common sense.

Well, the genie looked at Amal, and then he laughed. It was not a nice sound, but Amal was not daunted.

"Hah! You don't look very strong," sniggered the genie. "I shall win this contest easily," and he laughed again.

Amal picked up a stone.

"You must squeeze this stone until water comes out of it," he said, handing the genie the stone.

Well, the genie squeezed and squeezed, and huffed and puffed, but, of course, no water came out of the stone. He threw it down in a temper.

"Not possible!" he snapped.

Amal bent down and picked up the stone, and squeezed. And with a scrunching sound, liquid ran down Amal's fingers. The genie was astonished. And so would you have been if you had been there. What clever Amal had done was to put the egg in the same hand as the stone, and it was the egg that was broken. Genies are not terribly bright and this one was no exception.

Then Amal said, "Well, I win that one. But now perhaps you could crumble this stone into powder," and he handed the genie another stone. Well, the genie squeezed and squeezed, and huffed and puffed, but, of course, the stone did not crumble at all, not even the tiniest bit. The genie threw it down in a temper.

Amal picked it up and squeezed. And as he squeezed, powder fell from his fingers with a grinding sound. The genie was astonished. And so would you have been if you had been there, but you can guess what clever Amal had done. He put the salt in his hand as well as the stone.

The genie was feeling that his reputation was somewhat dented by Amal's performance so he needed to get his own back.

"You are clearly a great and mighty fighter," the genie said to Amal. "I should like to give you a meal to celebrate your achievements. Come and stay the night with me," and he smiled.

But Amal saw the smile, and kept his wits about him. After a dreadful meal, they both lay down to sleep in the genie's cave. Once Amal was sure the genie was asleep, he moved to the other side of the cave, leaving his pillow in the bed to look as if he were still there asleep. Then he watched. As the first light of dawn filtered into the cave, the genie woke up. He picked up a club, crept over to where he thought Amal was lying and pounded the club down onto the bed. Then he stomped out of the cave to fetch some water for his morning tea.

You can imagine his dismay when, on returning, he found Amal singing to himself as he lit the fire.

"Morning, genie! I thought I would get breakfast ready," said Amal cheerfully. "I hope you slept better than I did," he continued. "Some wretched insect batted me in the face during the night."

Well, at this the genie gave a great shriek and whistled himself as fast as possible into an old oil lamp that lay on the floor of the cave. He wasn't seen again for hundreds of years until a young lad called Aladdin happened to find the lamp.

The Girl who Owned a Bear

By L Frank Baum

Jane Gladys was amusing herself alone in the big sitting room upstairs. She was working on her first piece of embroidery – a sofa pillow for papa's birthday. The door opened and closed quietly. She raised her eyes and was astonished to find a strange man in the middle of the room.

He was short and fat, and was breathing heavily from climbing the stairs. He held a hat in one hand and underneath his other elbow was a good-sized book. He was dressed in a black suit that looked old and rather shabby.

"Excuse me," he said, while the child gazed at him in surprise. "Are you Jane Gladys Brown?"

"Yes, sir," she answered.

"Very good, very good, indeed!" he remarked.

"What do you want?" she asked.

"I'm going to be frank with you. Your father has treated me in a terrible manner."

Jane Gladys got off the windowsill and pointed her small finger at the door.

"Leave this room 'meejitly!" she cried, her voice trembling. "My papa is the best man in the world."

"Allow me to explain. I called on him the other day and asked him to buy the 'Complete Works of Peter Smith,' and what do you suppose he did?"

She said nothing.

"He ordered me from his office, and had me put out of the building by the janitor! I decided to be revenged. So, I'm going to present you with this book," he said, taking it from under his arm. Then he sat down, drew a fountain pen from his pocket and wrote her name in it.

After handing the book to her, he walked to the door, gave her a bow and left the room.

The child sat down in the window and glanced at the book. It had a red and yellow cover and the word 'Thingamajigs' was written across the front cover in big letters.

Then she opened it, curiously, and saw her name written in black letters upon the first white page.

She turned a page, and she had scarcely noted that it contained the picture of a monkey when the animal sprang from the book with a great crumpling of paper and landed upon the window seat beside her.

"He he he he he!" chattered the creature, springing to the girl's shoulder and then to the centre table. "This is great fun! Now I can be a real monkey instead of a picture of one."

"Real monkeys can't talk," said Jane Gladys.

"How do you know? Have you ever been one yourself?" inquired the animal, laughing loudly.

The girl was quite bewildered by this time. She thoughtlessly turned another page, and before she had time to look twice, there sprang over her shoulder a spotted leopard, which landed upon the

back of a big leather armchair
and turned to face her with a
fierce movement.

The monkey climbed to the top of the
chandelier and chattered with fright. The
leopard crouched upon the back of the
chair, lashed his tail from side to
side and glared at them.

"Which of us are you going to
attack first?" asked the monkey.

"I can't attack any of you," snarled the leopard.
"The artist made my mouth shut, so I haven't any
teeth, and he forgot to make my claws. But I'm a
frightful-looking creature, nevertheless, am I not?"

"I suppose you're frightful-looking enough. But
if you have no teeth nor claws we don't mind your
looks at all," said the monkey.

This annoyed the leopard so much that he

growled horribly, but the monkey just laughed.

Just then the book slipped from the girl's lap, and as she made a movement to catch it one of the pages near the back opened wide. She caught a glimpse of a fierce grizzly bear looking at her from the page, and quickly threw the book to the ground. It fell with a crash in the middle of the room, but beside it stood the great grizzly, who had wrenched himself from the page before the book had closed.

"Now," cried the leopard from his perch, "you'd better look out for yourselves! You can't laugh at him as you did at me. The bear has both claws and teeth."

"Indeed I have," said the bear, in a low, deep, growling voice. "And I know how to use them, too. If you read in that book you'll find that I eat little girls – shoes, dresses, ribbons and all!"

Jane Gladys was much frightened on hearing this, and she began to realize what the man meant when he said he gave her the book to be revenged.

"You mustn't eat me. It would be wrong."

"Why?" asked the bear, in surprise.

"Because I own you. The book was given to me, my name's on the front page. So you mustn't dare to eat your owner!"

The grizzly hesitated. "Then, of course, I can't

eat you," he decided. "That author is disappointing – as most authors are."

"The fault lies with all of you," said Jane Gladys, severely. "Why didn't you stay in the book, where you were put?"

The animals looked at each other.

"Now, you stupid creatures—"

But she was interrupted by them all making a rush for the book. There was a swish and a whirr and a rustling of leaves, and an instant later the book lay upon the floor looking just like any other book, while Jane Gladys' strange companions had all disappeared.

This story should teach us to think quickly and clearly upon all occasions, for had Jane Gladys not remembered that she owned the bear he probably would have eaten her before the bell rang.